RAINBOW RHINO

Written and illustrated by
Fox Carlton Hughes

Rainbow Rhino
Published by Ovation Books
P.O. Box 80107
Austin, TX 78758

For more information about our books, please write to us, call 512.478.2028, or visit our website at www.ovationbooks.net.

Distributed to the trade by National Book Network, Inc.

Library of Congress Cataloging-in-Publication available upon request.

ISBN-13: 978-0-9790275-3-6
ISBN-10: 0-9790275-3-5

To my dear wife, Peggy Ann, I
joyously dedicate this book.
Her unwavering belief in me
has given wings and direction
to my errant dreams.

Somewhere, far, far away, there lived a family of rhinoceros.

There was
Poppa Rhino,
and
Momma Rhino
and
their little boy…

...Homer.

Homer was a very good boy, but he was an odd-looking little fellow. The tusk on the end of his nose was at least five times bigger than normal. This really embarrassed Homer, especially since the kids at school teased him about it.

So, Homer played by himself most of the time.

One day at school, Homer tried to hide his tusk by putting a trash basket over it, but he couldn't see where he was going and began bumping into the other children.

"Look where you're going!" they shouted.

Poor Homer got so mixed up that he stumbled into the water cooler. It tipped over with a crash, and there he stood in the middle of a big puddle of water. He still couldn't see anything, but he could hear all the other kids laughing at him.

That evening, Poppa Rhino tried to cheer him up. "Don't feel bad about your tusk, Homer, just look at all these guys in the funnies. They're all different in their own way, and that's what makes them so very special...just like you."

When that didn't help, Momma Rhino baked his favorite dessert, rhubarb pie. Homer didn't even take a bite.

Finally, he excused himself and went upstairs to his room.

Homer looked in
his mirror and a
sad little rhino stared
back. "I wish I didn't have this big tusk," he
wailed and threw himself on his bed in tears.

When Momma Rhino went upstairs to check on him, she saw he had cried himself to sleep. "Oh dear," she said to Poppa Rhino. "He's so unhappy, and I don't think there's anything we can do."

The next day was Saturday. Homer woke up early and looked out the window. It had rained all night, but now the sun was shining brightly. Then, Homer saw something that made him forget all his troubles.

Just over the green meadows was the biggest, brightest rainbow he had ever seen. "Oh, wow!" he shouted. "I'm going to go say hello."

He quickly got dressed, slid down the banister, and headed for the kitchen. His mom was making pancakes, and he grabbed one as he shot by.

"Thanks, Mom. I'm going to see the rainbow!" he called, as the screen door banged behind him.

He galloped across the field as fast as his little legs could carry him. He jumped wide ditches, climbed over fences, and shot past some puzzled cows.
"Good morning, cows!" he shouted as he ran by.

Finally, he skidded to a stop in front of the most beautiful rainbow that he'd ever seen. Homer's heart pounded with excitement as he stared up, up, up in amazement. The colors were dazzling and went all the way up into the soft, white clouds.

He was just about to say hello when he heard someone crying. He looked quickly from side to side, but he didn't see anyone. "Who's there?" he called out. "Who's crying?"

"I am," sobbed a very sad voice. "Up here. It's me, the rainbow."

Then suddenly, Homer was splattered with big, wet rainbow tears.

Homer moved closer to have a better look. Sure enough, there was a hole in the rainbow. All the colors were gushing out onto the ground.

"Oh, no!" Homer gasped.

The rainbow gave a little sniffle. "I'm waiting for the Dew Fairies. They are the only ones who know how to fix me, but I don't think I can last that long. I'm already starting to fade."

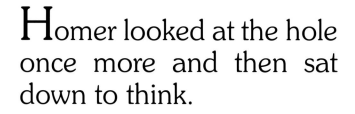

Homer looked at the hole once more and then sat down to think.

"There's got to be a way," he said. "There's just got to be!"

After a moment or two, he jumped up with a big grin and shouted, "Don't worry, Mr. Rainbow, I've got a great idea!"

Homer stepped back a few feet and turned to face the rainbow. He lowered his head and charged.

THUD-D-D !

Mr. Rainbow wasn't expecting anything like that and it made him sway from side to side.

When he looked down, he saw that Homer had rammed his oversized tusk into the hole. The leak had completely stopped!

"Homer!" shouted Mr. Rainbow. "You did it! Now I know I can hold out until the Dew Fairies get here."

Homer kept pushing with all his might. He stayed there all morning and all afternoon waiting for the Dew Fairies to arrive.

"I'm sure glad you have that wonderful big tusk, Homer. You must be very proud of it."

"Not really," said Homer. "The kids at school are always teasing me about it. They call me Homer the Homely."

Mr. Rainbow was thinking about Homer's problem when suddenly the Dew Fairies arrived. The air was filled with fluttering wings, silver needles and bright colored spiderweb silk as they started to stitch up the hole in Mr. Rainbow's side.

Meanwhile, a very tired Homer stretched out on the grass to rest.

GLUE

RAINBOW REPAIR

Mr. Rainbow was feeling much better now. "Thank you, Homer," he said. "You saved my life. Now I can come back again another day. And… you won't have to worry about the kids at school, anymore."

"How come?" asked Homer.

"Well," began Mr. Rainbow, "because of your kindness, something magical has happened. When you stopped the leak, all the colors somehow stuck to your tusk. You are now as beautiful as any rainbow in the sky.